APR 0 8 2011

# Attack of the Giant Flood

by **Kathryn Lay**        illustrated by **Jason Wolff**

magic Wagon

**visit us at www.abdopublishing.com**

Published by Magic Wagon, a division of the ABDO Group,
8000 West 78th Street, Edina, Minnesota 55439. Copyright
© 2011 by Abdo Consulting Group, Inc. International copyrights
reserved in all countries. All rights reserved. No part of this book
may be reproduced in any form without written permission from the
publisher.

Calico Chapter Books™ is a trademark and logo of Magic Wagon.

Printed in the United States of America, Melrose Park, Illinois.
032010
092010

 This book contains at least 10% recycled materials.

Text by Kathryn Lay
Illustrations by Jason Wolff
Edited by Stephanie Hedlund and Rochelle Baltzer
Cover and interior design by Abbey Fitzgerald

**Library of Congress Cataloging-in-Publication Data**
Lay, Kathryn.
  Attack of the giant flood / by Kathryn Lay ; illustrated by Jason
Wolff.
    p. cm. -- (Wendy's weather warriors ; bk. 5)
  Includes bibliographical references and index.
  ISBN 978-1-60270-758-0 (alk. paper)
  1. Floods--Juvenile literature. 2. Floods--Experiments--Juvenile
literature. I. Wolff, Jason, ill. II. Title.
  GB1399.L39 2010
  551.48'9--dc22
                            2009048826

# CONTENTS

CHAPTER 1: No Rain for Roses ........................... 4

CHAPTER 2: Rockets to the Clouds ..................... 12

CHAPTER 3: To Rain or Not to Rain .................... 18

CHAPTER 4: A Ceremony and a Surprise ............... 22

CHAPTER 5: Go Back! ..................................... 34

CHAPTER 6: Water Everywhere .......................... 38

CHAPTER 7: The Rescue .................................. 44

CHAPTER 8: Starring: Wendy's Weather Warriors ....... 51

CHAPTER 9: The Reward .................................. 57

CHAPTER 10: Let's Make a Movie ....................... 65

CHAPTER 11: Action! ..................................... 71

Did You Know? ............................................. 76

Flood Myths ............................................... 77

Dennis's Favorite Experiments .......................... 78

Safety Tips ............................................... 80

# CHAPTER 1

## No Rain for Roses

**W**endy bent down to the flowers in her mom's garden. The petals of the pink and purple petunias were drooping and looking brown. Even the buds on the rose bushes seemed afraid to open in such dry weather.

Wendy poured the water from her mom's watering can over them.

"The ground is so dry," her mother said. "I don't know when we've had such an abnormally dry spring. Not one drop of rain in almost six weeks."

Wendy gave the nearest flower the last of the water and stood. "We've been talking about it at school," she said. "Mr.

Andrews said that since it's the end of May and summer is almost here, it is going to be hard on everyone if we don't get rain soon."

Wendy's mom pointed to the grass. "We need to water the yard, but the city has us on strict watering rules. Only one hour in the early morning and evening every other day. And they will probably not even allow that if we don't get some rain soon."

Wendy went inside to sit beside her dad on the couch. He leaned forward, intently watching the meteorologist on television. Just as Wendy sat down, she heard the meteorologist say the word *rain*.

"Are we going to get some rain?" Wendy asked. She loved watching the weather with her dad, especially watching their favorite meteorologist. He was hardly ever wrong about a forecast. Of course, no one could completely predict every moment of the weather, especially in Texas.

Wendy's father nodded. "There's a possibility of some rain coming in by the end of the week. I wonder if I'll get to do any storm spotting."

Wendy's eyes opened wide. "Tornadoes?" she asked.

"Probably not," her father said. "But sometimes we get sudden heavy rain this time of year."

Wendy smiled. "But isn't that good? It's been too dry. Mom's flowers are dying. The grass looks almost yellow."

Her father clicked off the television. "We definitely need rain. But too much of a good thing can be dangerous."

Wendy knew what he was thinking about—floods. Where she used to live in East Texas, it flooded a lot when there were heavy rains. Once, they had to put sandbags on their back porch because the water was starting to come into their kitchen.

Now they were in the panhandle of Texas. They had all kinds of weather

there. It was time to do a little research on flooding in their area.

Wendy went into the backyard and into the Weather Warriors' clubhouse. It was really starting to look like a weather clubhouse. The walls were covered with pictures that Jessica had taken. There were pictures of the tornado that hit Circleville Elementary. And, there was a great shot of lightning over the soccer field during the big play-off game.

One of Wendy's favorite pictures was of the Weather Warriors standing beside the giant snowman they built during the snow party. Even Austin Scott was in the picture. It was thanks to his idea and his father's snow-making machine that they had the snow party.

The newest picture was of Mr. Andrews being dunked at the Hail to the King Spring Carnival.

Wendy sat down at the table where Dennis liked to work on his experiment ideas. Cumulus wandered into the clubhouse and put his paws on Wendy's leg.

"Hey, boy! You were the first member of Wendy's Weather Warriors."

The curly-haired Schnoodle barked as if to agree.

Wendy thumbed through the collection of books her father had given her at Christmas about weather around the United States. She looked up Amarillo, Texas, the closest big city to Circleville. It had lots to tell about the weather in that area. There was information about tornadoes, snow, hail, sleet, dust storms, heat, and lots about floods.

"Wow, they have some bad flash floods around here," she said, showing Cumulus the book. He put his nose on the open page and sniffed.

Wendy walked outside and looked at the rain gauge hanging on the clubhouse. It was dry and empty. She always kept a weather journal, but she hadn't been able to write down any notes from the rain gauge in weeks.

She hoped it really did rain soon. Circleville needed it. So did her mom's garden.

Then she remembered the dedication ceremony for the new middle school. The new principal was out of town, so Mr. Andrews had been asked to cut the ribbon at the ceremony. Mrs. Stuard and Mr. Rodriguez were taking vans full of kids from Circleville Elementary to cheer for him.

Wendy thought about the rain they needed. Maybe the big ceremony would be postponed if it rained.

She stared up at the fair weather clouds. She decided not to tell her mom she was hoping for a few more days of dry weather.

# CHAPTER 2

## Rockets to the Clouds

Class was louder than usual. Wendy could feel the excitement. School was ending in just a week. She had lots of plans for a fun summer, but she would miss being in Mr. Andrews's class.

"I can't wait to go to the lake," George Benson said. He put his hands together in a diving motion.

Jessica held out her camera. "My parents took me to the lake this weekend for a picnic. We walked around and I took pictures. It's really low. We talked with one of the park rangers. He said that boats were having trouble getting around small trees sticking out of the water."

Mr. Andrews tapped his ruler on his head. After several taps, the kids stopped talking. Wendy would miss Mr. Andrews's head tapping when he wasn't their teacher anymore. She wondered if he'd tap his head at the new middle school when he made announcements or walked down the halls as vice principal.

"I thought because everyone seems to be talking about the weather these days, we'd talk more about the dry weather. There's water all over Earth, in fact, more than seventy percent of our world is water. So what's the big deal about a few weeks without rain?"

"We need rain for the grass and plants and trees," Wendy said. "My mom's flowers need lots of water."

"And for the animals and the fish," Jessica added.

Dennis pulled out his notebook. "If we don't have rain, we could go into a drought and then we'd be in big trouble. I have this experiment where we can make it rain and . . ."

"But we can't make it rain," Dustin Burke said.

Mr. Andrews walked to the back of the classroom. He took out Leaping Larry, their new lizard, and held him carefully. Larry bobbed up and down like he was getting ready to leap, so Mr. Andrews put him back in his aquarium.

"Does anyone know what cloud seeding is?" Mr. Andrews took several wet wipes from a box on his desk and wiped his hands.

The room was quiet. Wendy knew the answer, but she hated being a know-it-all about weather. Finally, she raised her hand. "Cloud seeding is when . . ."

Austin jumped up. "It's when a farmer digs little holes in the clouds and plants seeds—maybe watermelon—for rain. Get it? Water . . . rain . . ."

Wendy groaned. "Like I was saying before I was rudely interrupted, cloud seeding can help bring more rainfall. The clouds are seeded by airplanes. They drop this special stuff into the clouds. And even rockets are sent up from the ground to help the rain come."

"Wow," the kids in Mr. Andrews's class said.

Mr. Andrews nodded. "Some people disagree with cloud seeding. But, for us, we're hoping for real rain in a few days. If we get enough, your mom's flowers should be fine, Wendy. But it'll take more than one rain event for the lake to rise very much."

Austin jumped up. Wendy rolled her eyes. Austin never raised his hand or waited for his turn. "I don't want it to rain. If it rains, I get stuck in the house and my mom says it's not good for me or for her when I'm stuck inside."

Wendy looked at Jessica. They had planned to go to the zoo, the city pool, and a baseball game that summer. But she knew they needed some rain. Soon.

Too bad they didn't have any of those special rockets lying around.

# CHAPTER 3

## To Rain or Not to Rain

Austin sat on the floor of the Weather Warriors' clubhouse and spun in a circle singing, "Rain, rain, go away, I want to go out and play."

It had started to rain for just a few minutes, then stopped like the sky had forgotten how. Wendy, Dennis, and Jessica were talking about the storm spotter meeting that summer. Dennis's and Jessica's parents had agreed they could go with Wendy and her family on the three-day trip.

Wendy looked at Austin's spinning. She hadn't decided yet if she was going to invite him to go.

Austin jumped up and grabbed Wendy's weather radio. "I want to listen to some music."

"That's a weather radio, Austin," Dennis said. He grabbed for the radio just as Austin flipped the switch on.

". . . eighty-percent chance of rain throughout the counties of Potter and Dyson on Saturday. Some of these storms moving in have the potential for isolated heavy rain and possible flash floods in low-lying areas . . ."

Wendy knew how bad floods could be. Especially flash floods in a low area. She wondered if people knew it could be dangerous.

"Do you think it'll rain during the ceremony?" Jessica asked. "Mr. Andrews asked me to take pictures. They might even hang them in the new school."

Wendy pushed her glasses up. They were always sliding down her nose. "I hope not. But if it rains a lot, they can have it another day."

Dennis shook his head. "Yeah, but then the new principal would be back and Mr. Andrews wouldn't get to cut the ribbon. It'll be the first middle school in Circleville. Just think, we'll be there with Mr. Andrews as vice principal. Maybe I could be in charge of weather experiments for the whole school."

Jessica took a picture of Dennis holding his notebook. "And maybe I could be the school photographer."

Wendy snapped her fingers. "Maybe we could have a weather club at the new school. We could tell people all about weather information and weather safety."

Austin jumped up and zoomed around the room. "Yeah, and I could . . ." He stopped zooming. "I could do something, I bet."

"Something silly," Jessica said.

"Mr. Andrews said that Mr. Rodriguez will drive us to the ceremony on Saturday, and then back to Circleville Elementary. The new middle school is just on the other side of town."

Wendy grinned. She couldn't wait for Saturday to come. She just hoped it wouldn't rain on the big ceremony.

She looked outside. There were a few altocumulus clouds. She grabbed her book on clouds. She read that altocumulus clouds meant the middle level of the atmosphere was cooling down and getting more moisture. Rain was coming soon.

## CHAPTER 4

## · A Ceremony and a Surprise ·

"Those clouds look like they're going to burst open with rain," Mr. Rodriguez said.

Wendy piled into the school van with Mr. Rodriguez, Miss Holland, Dennis, Jessica, and Austin. She was about to close the van door when Daniel Johnston ran up to the van.

"Mrs. Stuard says the other van is full and I need to ride with Mr. Rodriguez!" Daniel shouted. He jumped inside and grabbed the seat beside Austin.

"Hi, Austin," he said, waving his hand in front of Austin's nose.

Austin crossed his eyes. "Grrr," he said.

Wendy leaned against the window beside her seat and stared into the sky. The cumulonimbus clouds were piling high. Her heart pounded. If only the rain would wait until after the ceremony. It was Mr. Andrews's big day.

"Seat belts on," Mr. Rodriguez said, turning in the driver's seat. "That means everyone, Austin."

Finally, they were driving down the road behind the other two school vans. Mr. Andrews had to be at the ceremony early, so other teachers were driving his students to the lot where the new school was built.

Every Friday after school, Wendy's mom drove her to see the school. They hadn't been able to see it for two weeks, and now it was finished.

"I wonder what the inside of the school looks like," Jessica said, shouting over Austin's sudden burst of whistling.

Wendy shrugged. "Maybe they'll have some pictures of the plans," she said.

Not only was it Mr. Andrews's big moment as the vice principal, it would be their new school, too. It would be different in middle school. She hoped she would have classes with the other Weather Warriors. Even Austin could be fun.

"We're here," Mr. Rodriguez announced.

Wendy and the others pressed their faces against the windows. There were already lots of people standing beside a small stage in front of the school. On one side were tall trees in a fenced area.

"That's so cool that they didn't cut down the trees," Jessica said.

Dennis leaned forward in his seat. "My dad said the builders promised to keep the trees."

Wendy grinned. The school looked great. It had wide steps that led to tall wooden doors. The bricks were a dark red. There was a large sign for announcements. A smaller sign read, "We are a green school."

"Hey!" Austin yelled. "Look at that sign. The school isn't green. It's red!"

Jessica sighed. "Not that kind of green. The kind that means you do things for Earth. Recycling and using special lights and stuff."

When they got out of the van, Mr. Rodriguez and Miss Holland led them to where the other kids from Mr. Andrews's class waited.

Wendy's ponytail blew in the wind. The wind seemed a lot stronger than when they'd left Circleville Elementary. She rubbed her arm when she felt a few drops of rain.

Mr. Andrews stood beside two men in suits. One of the men was holding a giant pair of scissors. There was a big ribbon with a bow on it stretched across the front doors of the school.

"Mr. Andrews!" Wendy shouted. She jumped up and down and waved. Beside her, Jessica and Dennis did the same.

Their teacher looked toward them and smiled. Then one of the men in a suit stepped onto the small stage and up to a microphone.

"If I can get your attention please, we'll begin the ceremony now. It seems like the rain we've long hoped for is about to come, so we're going to have to hurry through this," the man said.

He introduced himself as the school superintendent. Then he introduced the man beside him, City Councilman Ford, and Mr. Andrews.

Mr. Andrews stepped up to the microphone and cleared his throat. "Thank you all for coming to the dedication ceremony for Circleville's first middle school, Cyclone Middle School. I'm especially excited about seeing my fifth grade students from Circleville Elementary." He waved at them.

"Mr. Thomas, our principal, couldn't be here today. I'm honored to let you know that he and I have met many times and we are excited about the possibilities for the new school."

"Yay!" Austin shouted.

"Among the many things that I'd like to see happen someday at the new school, one is to have a weather lab. This is something that several of my students have influenced me to think about because of the important part they have played in weather safety at Circleville Elementary. When the money is available, I'll push for this to be added here at Cyclone Middle School."

Wendy gasped. "A weather lab," she whispered to Jessica and Dennis. They stared at her with wide eyes. Mr. Andrews had kept this surprise a secret.

"So today, we dedicate Cyclone Middle School for all the students who pass through its halls," Mr. Andrews said.

He took the scissors from the superintendent and stepped in front of the ribbon. He posed with the scissors ready to cut as Jessica moved forward and took their picture. She stood beside a photographer from the *Circleville Times*. The photographer snapped pictures of Mr. Andrews, then smiled at Jessica and shook her hand.

With a quick motion, Mr. Andrews cut the ribbon. As it separated, everyone applauded and shouted. Mr. Andrews and the two men pointed to the front doors of the school. Jessica and the other photographer took more pictures.

Wendy clapped until her hands stung. She couldn't wait to see the inside of the school.

"As special invited guests," the superintendent said, "we'll take a quick tour of the school. Remember that classroom desks and library books have not been added yet."

A boom of thunder exploded over them and rain suddenly dropped from the skies. Everyone moved inside the school.

Jessica took pictures of the halls, the office, the glass cases for trophies, the library that would soon be filled with books and posters, the empty classrooms, the cafeteria, and the auditorium.

"Wow," Dennis said. "We have an auditorium that doesn't smell like taco surprise."

As they passed windows, Wendy saw rain running down the glass outside. She was glad they were inside.

When the tour was finished, Wendy and her friends laughed as they ran for the school van. The rain had slowed, but water covered the sidewalk and they sloshed through puddles.

Mr. Rodriguez and Miss Holland jumped inside the van.

"Well, the ceremony has ended along with the dry weather," the vice principal said. "It's time to get you back to school to meet your parents." With a glance back in the rearview mirror he said, "I know a shortcut back to the school. We'll drive down Old River Road and get there before everyone else."

Wendy stopped talking to Jessica. "Where's Old River Road?" she asked her friends.

Dennis rubbed his fingers against the glass of the windows as the rain ran down the outside. "It's a road that runs down beside a dry river. My dad said he used to catch frogs there. But it's almost always dry now."

Wendy's heart pounded. She watched the rain falling in buckets. It was raining hard and fast. Too fast.

"What do you mean, down beside a dry river?" she asked.

Dennis stared at her a moment. "Uh-oh. The road runs beside the riverbed, below the main road and the bridge that crosses over the old river."

Wendy opened her mouth to tell Mr. Rodriguez he was driving them right into danger.

# CHAPTER 5

## Go Back!

The pounding rain slowed as they drove across town, through streets that Wendy didn't remember seeing before. The streets were getting smaller and the water ran across the road in front of the van.

"Shouldn't we go back the same way we came?" she asked Mr. Rodriguez.

"This is a shortcut," he replied. "We'll be back at Circleville Elementary before you know it."

Wendy leaned forward and said, "Could you turn the radio on, please? We should be listening in case they say anything about the weather."

Daniel said, "It's barely even raining now. You weather kids are just weird."

"Weather Warriors," Jessica corrected.

"And we're not weird, we're careful," Wendy said.

Mr. Rodriguez switched on the radio. Miss Holland turned the knob until a voice said, "Remember that flash flooding can happen at any time in rain this heavy. The storm is slowing, but with this rainfall rate, low-lying areas can be treacherous. There has been a flash flood warning issued for Dyson County until three PM."

Wendy gripped the back of Mr. Rodriguez's seat. "I really think we shouldn't take the Old River Road. Did you know it only takes two feet of water to move a car?"

"That's silly," Austin said. "This van weighs a lot. I bet it weighs more than an

elephant. I saw elephants walking through rivers on a television show."

Wendy glared at him. "Flash floods mean really fast-moving water."

Mr. Rodriguez glanced at her from the rearview mirror.

Dennis held out his notebook. "I saw an experiment once where there was this little pretend city and stuff. You could press a button and WHOOSH, water suddenly came in and knocked over little cars and crashed into the buildings."

Jessica whispered, "I don't want to take pictures of the van stuck in water."

Mr. Rodriguez slowed to a stop. "Maybe you're right. We can turn back and take the bridge that crosses over Old River Road. It'll take us back to the main road."

Miss Holland said, "I think that's a good idea, Marshall."

Wendy leaned back in her seat and let out her breath. She hadn't realized how hard her heart had been pounding.

## CHAPTER 6

## Water Everywhere

"**W**hat's that loud noise?" Austin asked. He pushed open the window by his seat.

Wendy heard it, too. It was a roaring sound, like a waterfall.

Just as Mr. Rodriguez drove the van onto the bridge, everyone gasped. A few feet below the bridge, water rushed along the ground. It pushed past small trees and bushes and smashed against large rocks.

Mr. Rodriguez drove slowly. "I've never seen so much water in that old river. Not for a lot of years anyway."

"That's because it's dry most of the time," Jessica said. "My grandpa took me out here once. I took pictures of bugs and butterflies and wildflowers. But no water."

Wendy's eyes went wide. "Stop the van!" she screamed.

Mr. Rodriguez slowed the van to a stop. "Wendy Peters, you shouldn't yell at the driver like that. It's very dangerous. I could've had an accident."

Wendy pointed out Mr. Rodriguez's window. "But look down there, in the water. It's a car!"

Below them, caught in the rushing flood water, a bright green car seemed to be riding the waves. Wendy could see someone inside, waving out the window.

Suddenly the car turned sideways and pushed against a large rock in the middle of the rushing water. It stuck there while the water rushed all around it.

A man began crawling out the window of the car. Halfway out, he felt forward into the water.

"He's going to be swept away!" Wendy shouted.

But the man was still hanging on to the car door. Everyone jumped out of the van.

"Stay away from the bridge railing!" Mr. Rodriguez shouted. "That water is moving very fast down there."

Wendy could see the man was struggling to hold on. Finally, he kicked his foot against the rock and pushed himself onto the hood of the car.

"Climb on your roof!" Wendy shouted. She remembered that in a flood you should be at the highest spot possible.

Right now, the only high spot for this man was the top of his car.

When he didn't move, everyone shouted together, "Climb on the roof of your car, Mister!"

Wendy nudged Jessica. "Take pictures."

Jessica grabbed her camera from around her neck and started snapping pictures.

Wendy waved at the man standing on his car. They had to get him help. The water seemed to move faster and higher.

"Look, the inside of his car is starting to fill with water," Mr. Rodriguez said. "If it gets much higher, it'll knock him into the flood."

"Call 9-1-1!" Wendy shouted.

Mr. Rodriguez pulled a cell phone from his pocket. After a moment, he was yelling over the sound of the rushing water. He quickly told the emergency services operator what bridge they were on.

"They're on their way," he said.

Wendy's heart pounded. That could have been them trapped inside or forced to climb on top of the van.

"Why is the water still so high and so fast?" Daniel asked. "It stopped raining."

Dennis said, "Remember the experiment I told about? A flash flood comes from all the rain we had before."

Wendy nodded. "And that road down there is really low and right beside that old river."

From the distance, Wendy could hear sirens coming. She waved at the man standing on his car. She hoped he could hear them, too.

Just as he waved back, water started to flow over the top of the car. As if in slow motion, the man slipped and fell toward the rising water.

# CHAPTER 7

## The Rescue

Wendy and Jessica grabbed each other's arms. The man grabbed onto the edge of the roof as he slid. One leg was in the water, but he threw the other over the roof and with both hands clung to the edges of the car roof.

Wendy and the others jumped up and down and waved as a police car, ambulance, and fire truck drove onto the bridge. From above came the sudden whirring sound of a helicopter.

"Cool!" Austin shouted, spinning around like helicopter blades.

Mr. Rodriguez ran over to the police car. As men and women stepped out of the police car, fire truck, and ambulance, the helicopter hovered over the flooded road.

Wendy held her breath as a man sitting on the side of the helicopter pushed off and into the air. He was attached to a cable that lowered him slowly toward the man hanging on to the car.

"This is exciting," Daniel said.

Wendy glared at him. "It's not exciting, it's horrible. That man should not have driven down that road."

"Maybe he didn't listen to the warnings," Dennis said.

Jessica snapped picture after picture of the rescue. "Well, he should have. That's why they have them."

Mr. Rodriguez and Miss Holland were talking with the emergency workers. They walked back to the group from Mr. Andrews's class.

"It's a good thing we took this bridge, or no one might have seen this guy," Mr. Rodriguez said. He gave them a tired smile. "If it wasn't for you kids, we might have been down there hoping for rescue."

Austin rolled his head back and forth. "Yeah, and we could've flown up to the helicopter like we were in the circus."

Everyone watched as the rescue worker came closer to the man on the car. The man reached up as his rescuer reached down. They grabbed each other by the hand.

Wendy could hear the rescue worker shouting, but she couldn't understand what he was saying. Finally, the man pulled his rescuer close enough for the rescuer to throw a looped belt over him.

Wendy held her breath as the rescue worker and the man were pulled slowly up toward the helicopter. Below them the

water kept rushing. With a sudden jolt, the car was pushed free from the rocks and swept away. The group watched as the car shot down the quick-moving waters until it slammed against a tree.

"Boy, that was close," Austin said.

Wendy didn't think he was still imagining how fun it would be riding up to the helicopter.

"He's almost in!" Jessica shouted. She pointed her camera at the helicopter just as hands reached out and pulled the rescuer inside. Then more hands pulled in the stranded man.

The ambulance and fire truck drove away. A police officer walked over to the group standing beside the school van.

"My name is Officer Deur. That man has a lot to be thankful for tonight," she said. "It's a good thing you were crossing when you did."

Mr. Rodriguez pointed to Wendy. "This young lady, Wendy, and her friends are the same Weather Warriors who warned Circleville Elementary about the tornado before it hit. And they've helped many times with other weather information. They warned me not to take the Old River Road or we'd have been down there needing rescue."

The police officer smiled. She pulled out a notepad. "I'd like to get all of your names."

"Oh no!" Austin shouted. "We're going to be arrested." He threw his hands in the air.

With a laugh Officer Deur said, "I think that man on that helicopter would love to know who to thank."

As she began writing down their names, a large white van drove onto the bridge. Two men jumped out. One carried a large camera. On the side of the van were big leaders that read, "KRLM, Channel 6 News."

"We heard about the rescue. Did we miss it?" the reporter shouted.

Officer Deur nodded. "Afraid so. But I know you'll enjoy interviewing these young people. They are the real heroes today."

Wendy cleared her throat as the cameraman turned toward her.

# CHAPTER 8

## Starring: Wendy's Weather Warriors

"**H**urry, the news is almost on!" Wendy shouted.

Her mother passed around the last of the popcorn. "I feel like we're at the movies," she said with a laugh.

Wendy sat between Dennis and Jessica. Austin sat cross-legged on a cushion beside Dennis. Cumulus was curled in his lap, snoring as if they had a crowd of people in their living room every evening.

Wendy's parents sat on the couch with Dennis's dad. Jessica's parents and Austin's parents were sitting in kitchen chairs behind the couch. Even Dennis's older brother and Austin's little sister were there.

"Ssh!" Wendy ordered when the commercial about cleaner and brighter clothes ended.

"Tonight," the news announcer said, "we have clips from yesterday's dramatic high water rescue at the Old River Road. And thanks to a van full of schoolkids and their teachers, a man was rescued from the flash flooding that came with the sudden rain yesterday afternoon."

Jessica pulled out her camera and took a picture of the television.

"We have some amazing amateur footage of the rescue that was shot from a firefighter's cell phone," the reporter said.

"Hey, look! It's that man!" Dennis shouted, pointing at the television.

Wendy clapped her hands. "Wow, I didn't know it was being filmed."

They watched as the helicopter hovered over the man and lowered the rescue worker to him. Wendy knew the man would be rescued, but her heart still pounded as the two men were lifted into the helicopter.

Wendy's dad whistled. "That was some rescue." He bent over and rubbed Wendy's head. "That man has you all to thank for it."

The news video switched to the interview the reporter did with Wendy and the others.

"I'm told, young lady, that you warned your teacher not to drive down that very same road," the reporter said. He tilted the microphone at Wendy.

"Flash floods kill lots of people," Wendy said, smiling at the camera. "We just did what the Weather Warriors do. We warn and inform people about weather."

The reporter asked Wendy all about the Weather Warriors and then interviewed the others. Austin said hello to everyone he knew and made faces into the camera.

At the end of the interviews, the news announcer saluted the camera. "This is Dill Wilkerson giving a big salute to the kids and adults from Circleville Elementary and their quick thinking. And a special salute to those Weather Warriors."

Wendy's mom turned off the television. "It's time to honor our heroes with a pizza party," she said.

Everyone clapped and shouted just as the phone rang.

"Peters' residence," Wendy's father said into the phone. He nodded and said, "Yes, they are all here. Really? Well thank you, I know they'll be thrilled."

He hung up the phone.

"Who was that?" Wendy asked.

Her father smiled. "That was the man you rescued. He wants to meet the four of you, plus Mr. Rodriguez, Miss Holland, and the other kid at school tomorrow." He winked at them. "It seems that he wants to give you all a reward."

# CHAPTER 9

## The Reward

**M**r. Andrews walked up and down the aisles as he talked about the three branches of government. Bob the Boa was wrapped around his arm, his tongue going in and out, catching the smells around him.

"Remember for this week's project, I want you to make a poster of the legislative, executive, and judicial branches and tell who is in charge and what they do. Be creative."

Larry Davis raised his hand. "Mr. Andrews, did you see the news last night? Did you see Wendy and Dennis and Jessica and Daniel and . . ."

"And me!" Austin shouted.

Mr. Andrews nodded. "Yes, I saw Mr. Rodriguez and everyone. He told me this morning that he is glad the Weather Warriors were in his van."

Austin jumped up and waved his hand. "And guess what? We're going to get an award."

Wendy raised her hand. "He means a reward. It's from the man who was in the car in the water."

Mr. Andrews slipped Bob back into his aquarium. "I heard about that from Mrs. Stuard. You all deserve it."

Jessica said, "We're meeting in Mr. Rodriguez's office today after school. Can you come, too?"

"I'd be happy to be there," Mr. Andrews said. "Now, let's get back to social studies."

Wendy tried to concentrate on the branches of the government, but she kept thinking about the reward they would be getting. Would it be money? She didn't think her parents would let her accept money for saving someone's life. Maybe it was a trip to Disney World or a big party at the pool that summer?

At lunch, Wendy, Dennis, and Jessica sat in their usual spots together. Wendy traded lunch boxes with Jessica, who traded with Dennis. They all closed their eyes and opened them.

"Cool," Dennis said. "Turkey on an onion roll. Now I can breathe in Austin's face and make him pass out."

Jessica giggled. "I don't think anything would make him faint." She sniffed the plastic bag in the lunch she'd gotten from Dennis. "Looks like you made your own lunch again. A hot dog sandwich with grape jelly on top." She made a face. "Why do you have to put grape jelly on everything?"

Wendy was glad she traded with Jessica. The roast beef and cheese sandwich looked great. She took a big bite. It tasted as good as it looked.

"Hey, I want to trade, too!" Austin shouted as he ran over and bounced into the seat across from Dennis.

Jessica said, "You can have mine." She grabbed Austin's lunch. Even school meat loaf looked better than Dennis's sandwiches.

They were almost done eating when Mr. Andrews walked over and said, "Mrs. Stuard wants to talk with you. The man who you rescued has to leave town this afternoon and wants to give you all your reward now. I've already sent Daniel to Mr. Rodriguez's office. Come with me."

Wendy and her friends cleaned up their table, then they followed Mr. Andrews to the school office. They waved at the secretary, who was eating carrots and celery sticks.

"They are waiting for you in Mr. Rodriguez's office," she mumbled.

The group squeezed into the vice principal's office. Wendy, Jessica, Dennis, and Austin joined Mr. Rodriguez, Mrs. Stuard, Mr. Andrews, Daniel, and a man in a brown suit with a green tie.

The man smiled. Wendy smiled back. He'd been too far away to see his face when he was standing on his car, but she had watched him on the news interview.

Mrs. Stuard said, "Mr. Petrey only has a few minutes before he leaves on a business trip out of town. I told him our heroes could miss a few minutes of class."

The man said, "Yes, I couldn't wait to meet each of you." He shook hands with everyone in the office. "There is no way I can tell you how grateful I am for what you did. It was a mistake for me to take that road. I was in a hurry and I thought the shortcut would be faster."

Mr. Rodriguez cleared his throat. "Well, we all make mistakes. Sometimes we need help to show us the right way." He smiled at Wendy.

Mr. Petrey nodded. "I own a business and have a bit of money set aside. I heard that you kids were on your way back from a special ceremony for your new middle school."

Wendy nodded. "That will be our school next year. And our teacher, Mr. Andrews, will be vice principal."

"Yes, I spoke with him earlier. We talked about your new school and some of his dreams," Mr. Petrey said. "As part of your reward, I'd like to help build the weather lab he wants for the school."

Wendy clapped her hands. Jessica snapped a picture of Mr. Petrey. Dennis pulled out his famous weather experiment notebook to show the man. Mr. Andrews's eyes opened wide.

"And for each of you who were there to make sure I was rescued, I've got free passes to the new water park for you and your family."

Austin shouted, "Splash!"

Wendy grinned at Austin. "Splash," she repeated.

That was one flood of water they were all going to love.

# CHAPTER 10

## Let's Make a Movie

**W**endy sat cross-legged on her bed, her weather journal on her lap. She tapped her pen against her lips. Cumulus snored loudly beside her, curled up on her pillow.

Like all her friends, she was excited about the reward Mr. Petrey gave them. It wasn't just for them, but for everyone who would be going to Cyclone Middle School. But they hadn't helped the man get rescued for a reward. And they had come close to needing rescue, too.

Wendy bet that lots of people didn't know how dangerous it was driving through a low area when there might be flash flooding. Lots of people drove through high water and got stuck or swept away.

"We have to warn them," she told Cumulus. "Really warn them!"

Wendy snapped her fingers. She had an idea. And she needed the Weather Warriors' help.

Wendy jumped off her bed and ran into the hall. She called Jessica's house first.

"Hi," Jessica said.

Wendy paced as she talked. "Jessica, we need to have a Weather Warriors meeting at your house."

Jessica gasped. "Really? Oh boy, I'll ask my mom."

"Wait," Wendy said. "We need to do it when your dad is there."

"My dad?" Jessica asked.

"I have an important idea and we need your dad's help," Wendy explained.

When she said good-bye to Jessica, she called Dennis and told him to meet her at Jessica's house. Then she took a deep breath and called Austin.

Wendy rode her bicycle the two blocks to Jessica's house. Her stuffed backpack bounced against her back.

By the time she got to Jessica's house, her breath came in gasps. She laid her bike on Jessica's front yard, ran onto the porch, and rang the doorbell.

"Come in," Jessica said when she opened the door. "Everyone is here and we're dying to hear your idea."

Wendy followed Jessica to the kitchen. Dennis and Austin sat at the kitchen table munching on bowls of granola. Mr. Roberts leaned against a counter, listening to Dennis talk about his weather experiments.

"Hi, pokey," Austin said. He chewed a handful of granola mix and opened his mouth to show Wendy.

"Gross," she said.

She waved at Jessica's dad. "Thanks for coming to our meeting, Mr. Roberts. We need your help because you are a reporter at the news station."

Mr. Roberts smiled. "I hope I can help you. What's your idea?"

Wendy unzipped her backpack and pulled out a video camera, her weather notebook, and a folded poster. She opened the poster. In big red letters it read *Flash Flood Safety Video by Wendy's Weather Warriors*.

Wendy picked up the video camera. "We need to tell everyone in Circleville about safety during floods. Especially when there is a danger of flash floods."

Mr. Roberts nodded. "That's a great idea, Wendy. I'm sure I can get my boss to show a short clip of it on the news."

Wendy frowned. "Not the whole video?"

Jessica's father shook his head. "It would have to be very short. But if we showed a clip and told about it, you could tell people how to contact you to get a copy."

"A copy?" Wendy said. She snapped her fingers. "That's another great idea. We could make copies and sell them. My dad has a machine to do that. And we could sell them cheap so everyone would buy one."

Austin jumped up. "I'm going to be a movie star!" he shouted.

Wendy thought Austin would be great to play the part of a flash flood. He was always moving fast.

# CHAPTER 11

## Action!

"**A**re we ready?" Wendy asked. "Flash Flood Safety, take one!"

Wendy swung the video camera around Jessica's backyard. She focused in on Dennis sitting in a big plastic toy car.

"Hmm, I think I'll go this way," he said. "This road is faster."

Wendy shouted into the microphone. "There is a flash flood warning for your county. Get to higher ground. Don't drive in high water or low areas. Don't walk in flooded streets. Don't walk near flooded storm drains. And *don't* ignore this warning!"

Dennis pretended to turn off the radio. He pedaled the car off the sidewalk and onto the grass.

Just then, Austin ran out from behind a tree. He wore a big sign that read, Flash Flood Freddy. He jumped and twirled and ran around Dennis and his toy car. He pushed the car while Dennis shouted, "Help, Flash Flood Freddy is attacking!" Finally, Austin sat on the hood of the little car and stopped it from moving.

Jessica stepped in front of the camera. "This driver didn't pay attention to the weather warnings. And now he's trapped by the flood."

"Cut!" Wendy shouted. "That was perfect."

Dennis said, "Now, it's my turn to do the flash flood experiment."

He ran over to a sandbox where he'd built a little town of plastic toys. As Wendy filmed, he explained about rain and flooding as he used a watering can to pour rain over the town. Then he talked about flash floods, grabbed a bucket full of water, and dumped it into the edge of the sandbox.

The water flowed quickly through the roads he had built. It filled the rivers and the lake. Soon, little toy people and cars and trees were floating in the water.

"And that's what a flash flood can do," he explained with a bow.

Wendy moved the camera to where Jessica held up pictures of floods she had printed from her computer.

Finally, Wendy gave Jessica the camera. She cleared her throat and read from all her notes about flood safety.

She turned as she heard clapping. Mr. Andrews and Mr. Roberts were standing on the porch.

"Excellent," Mr. Andrews said. "I'm glad I came to watch. I know everyone in Circleville will be helped because of that video. I'm going to talk to the school superintendent. I'm recommending that we have a showing of it at every school for the kids, their parents, the teachers, and anyone who wants to come."

"Wow," Wendy said. The Weather Warriors had their own video.

Dennis tapped Wendy's shoulder. "Hey, that other guy in our van on Saturday, Daniel, he wants to know if he can join our club."

Mr. Andrews said, "Melissa Gibbs asked me yesterday if anyone could join, too."

Wendy pushed up her glasses.  She snapped her fingers. "I think my dad and I have a new summer project," she said.

Jessica hung her camera strap on her wrist.  "What kind of project?" she asked.

Wendy said, "We're going to make the weather clubhouse bigger."

"Bigger?" Dennis asked.

Wendy nodded.  "Bigger."  She had a feeling they were about to have a flood of new warriors.

# Did You Know?

Flooding can happen at any time during heavy rains. Floods can happen suddenly in a low-lying dry area when heavy rain comes. Flash floods are floods that happen quickly. Flash floods are the number one weather-related killer in the United States.

A Flood Watch or Flash Flood Watch means that flooding might happen soon. You should listen to the radio or television news for information. If you hear a warning of a flash flood, immediately tell an adult.

During a Flood Warning, you might be asked to leave the area and get to higher ground.

A Flash Flood Warning is serious. It means a flash flood is happening now. Tell an adult and get to high ground right away.

# Flood Myths

**MYTH:** Flash floods only happen right when it's raining.

**FACT:** This is one of the most dangerous myths about flash floods. If rain is coming down heavily, a flash flood can flow down a dry creek bed or gulch. Although this kind of flooding often happens in the southwest, it can also happen anywhere there is a path for water to flow into a low area from a higher elevation.

**MYTH:** If you know what a street or a dry creek area looks like normally, you also know how much water you will be going through during a flood.

**FACT:** You cannot know for sure if a roadway is still the same under rushing water. Rushing waters may damage the road. Do not try to drive across any flooded road or area where you cannot see the bottom.

# DENNIS'S Favorite Experiments

This project will take a little time to create. Line the box with the garbage bag and put sand or dirt several inches thick in it. Build a city in the dirt with higher areas around it. Make small hills and mountains out of clay. Glue down the houses and buildings, but not the people, cars, animals, and trees.

## YOU NEED:

- A long cardboard box
- A garbage bag
- Dirt or sand
- Clay
- A collection of toy houses, cars, trees, people, etc.
- Glue
- An empty bucket
- A watering can full of water

Begin by pouring a small amount of water over your miniature city with the watering can. This represents rain. After a while, pour the rest of the water into the bucket. Keep pouring until the bucket is nearly full. Then quickly dump the bucket's water at the edge of the town.

Describe what happens to the people, cars, animals, and trees. What about the houses? Did the water raise high around them? Did it cover them?

# Safety Tips

1. If you are outdoors and hear flood warnings, immediately look for shelter on the highest ground possible. Don't go near rivers, streams, or ponds. Storm drains are dangerous because the area around them may flood when the water doesn't drain fast enough. Never walk through floodwater higher than your calves.

2. If you are inside, get to the highest place in the building. Tell an adult to take water, blankets, food, and a battery-powered radio.

3. If you are in a car and water is rising, get out of the car and move to higher ground immediately.

4. Prepare a disaster plan with your family. Have a disaster supply kit in both your home and car that includes a first aid kit, bottled water, flashlights, and a battery-operated radio. Check disaster Web sites for more things to include in your kits.

5. If you live in an area that has flooded, drink bottled water or boiled water until you are told it is safe to drink fresh water. Do not use any electrical equipment that has not first been dried and checked.